BRAVE LITTLE MONSTER

BRAVE LITTLE MONSTER

by **Ken Baker**

illustrated by
Geoffrey Hayes

SCHOLASTIC INC.
New York Toronto London Auckland Sydney
Mexico City New Delhi Hong Kong Buenos Aires

Albert couldn't sleep. Goose bumps covered his hairy arms. His fangs chattered. He shivered with fright.

Even though Albert's mom had told him there were no such things as little girls and boys, he knew better.

Albert knew that scary boys and girls love to hide in little monsters' rooms at night.

Albert saw something move in his closet. It looked like a scary little girl eating an ice-cream cone. She was probably dripping ice cream all over Albert's clothes.

Albert knew that's what little girls do. They think it's funny to drip ice cream all over your clothes.

It makes them laugh so hard that their bellies hurt. And when they're done laughing, they

EAT YOU UP!

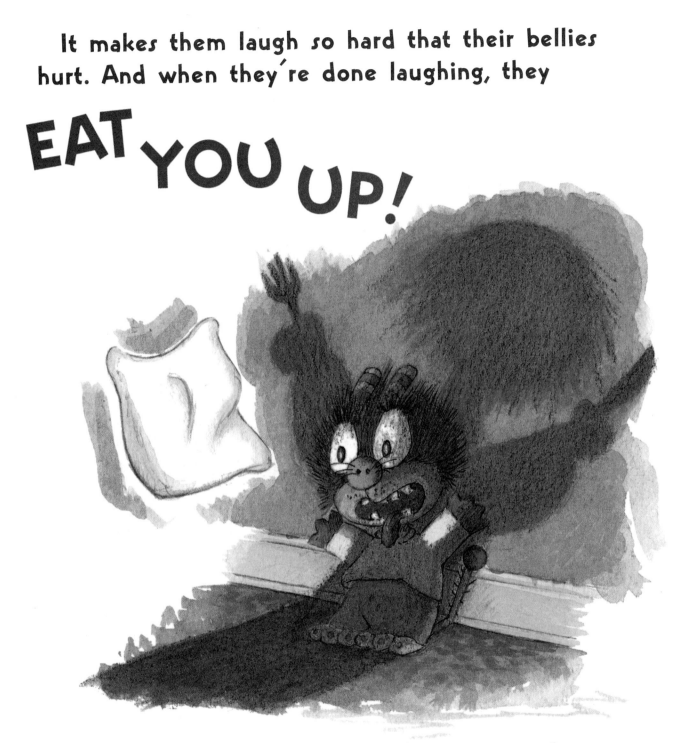

Little girls love to eat little monsters after they've had a good belly-busting laugh.

Albert yelled. "Help me! There's a little girl in my closet. She's spilling ice cream on my clothes and wants to eat me up."

"Go to sleep, Albert," his mom shouted from downstairs. "There's no such thing as a little girl."

Albert sighed. He would have to get rid of the little girl himself. He picked up one of his smelly socks off the floor

and threw it at the closet.

"Get out of my closet, you good-for-nothing, scary little girl, or I'll throw an even smellier sock at you," yelled Albert.

There was no answer. Albert thought he must have scared her away. Little girls can't stand the smell of monster socks. Albert just hoped she hadn't spilled too much ice cream on his clothes.

Finally, Albert felt safe. Except
now he had to go to the bathroom.
He had to go monstrously bad,
but he didn't dare get out of bed.
He was sure there was a mean little
boy under his bed coloring in a
coloring book. Albert could hear
his crayons squeaking.

But if you ever try to get out of bed, they grab your feet and play piggie on each one of your hairy little monster toes until you can't stand it.

Then they

EAT YOU UP!

"Mom!" Albert yelled. "There's a little boy coloring under my bed who wants to play piggie on my hairy little toes."

Albert's mom poked her head in his room.
"Albert," she said firmly. "It's getting late.
For the last time, there are no such things as
little boys and girls! Now close your eyes and
go to sleep."

Albert was on his own. He knew there was only one way to deal with little boys that hide under your bed. He closed his eyes and put his head under the bed. He stuck out his slobbery, hairy tongue and went,

"PHHHBPT!"

He counted to five.
When Albert opened his eyes the little boy was gone, but Albert thought he saw a coloring book under his bed.

Albert hopped out of bed and ran all the way to the bathroom.

When he came back, he flipped his bedroom light on and off to see if the little boy and girl had come back. There was no sign of them. Albert jumped into bed. He hoped they weren't still hiding somewhere in his room.

Albert had just closed his eyes when he thought he heard a quiet laugh come from his window. He sat up. Through the curtains, he saw the little girl and boy dancing and doing somersaults.

Albert recognized the dance that the little
boy and girl were doing. It was the hungry
dance. Albert knew they would laugh and
giggle all night long doing the hungry dance.
When they were good and hungry, they would

EAT ALBERT UP!

Albert had to get rid of the little
girl and boy once and for all. His heart
pounded as he climbed out of bed.
He trembled as he walked toward the
curtains where the children twirled and
jumped.

With his nose almost touching the curtains, Albert shouted as loud as he could,

"Little boy and girl, stop doing the hungry dance and go home! You're not going to eat this little monster for dinner!"

Then Albert took a deep breath and threw open the curtains. There was no little boy or girl. He could only see the big tree waving in the wind. He smiled. The little girl and boy were finally gone!

Albert skipped across the room and leapt back into bed. He knew there were no more scary little boys and girls in his room. He had chased them away all by himself.

Albert had almost fallen asleep when he felt his mom's hairy lips give him a soft, slobbery kiss on the cheek.

"Good night, my brave little monster," she whispered. "Sleep tight."

For Denise,
my greatest friend
—K.B.

ISBN 0-439-43680-X

Text copyright © 2001 by Ken Baker.
Illustrations copyright © 2001 by Geoffrey Hayes.
All rights reserved.
Published by Scholastic Inc., 557 Broadway, New York, NY 10012,
by arrangement with HarperCollins Publishers.
SCHOLASTIC and associated logos are trademarks and/or
registered trademarks of Scholastic Inc.

12 11 10 9 8 7 6 5 4 3 2   2 3 4 5 6 7/0

Printed in the U.S.A.   24

First Scholastic printing, September 2002

Design by Carla Weise